IV

THE FARMER AND THE FAIRY

AND OTHER STORIES

This edition published in 2016 by Pikku Publishing
7 High Street
Barkway
Hertfordshire SG8 8EA
www.pikkupublishing.com

ISBN: 978-0-9934884-2-9

First published by the University of London Press Ltd in 1936

Pikku Publishing and Dr Frances Grundy, heir to the estate of
Elizabeth Clark, wish to state that they have used all reasonable
endeavours to establish copyright. If you would like to contact
the Publisher, please write to Pikku Publishing.

1 3 5 7 9 10 8 6 4 2

Printed in China by Toppan Leefung Printing Ltd

THE MESSENGER BEGGED YOGODAGU TO FLY.

(See page 14)

[Frontispiece

THE FARMER AND
THE FAIRY

AND OTHER STORIES

by

ELIZABETH CLARK

Author of "Twenty Tales for Telling,"
"Tales for Jack and Jane," etc.

Illustrated by

NINA K. BRISLEY

Pikku Publishing

AUTHOR'S NOTE

The tales in this little book and its companions are reprinted from various collections of stories for storytellers which I have written during the past ten years.

It has been very often suggested to me that children would enjoy reading these stories quite as much as (I am happy to believe) they have hitherto enjoyed hearing them read or told. Accordingly, some of the stories have been chosen.

I hope that these small books may bring pleasure to innumerable small people, at home, at school, or wherever they and the books may be.

ELIZABETH CLARK

CONTENTS

Chapter One : The Captive Bee

> A Swarm of Bees in May
> Is worth a Load of Hay.
> A Swarm of Bees in June
> Is worth a Silver Spoon.
> But a Swarm in July—
> You had best let 'em fly !

THAT is an English rhyme about bees, and it makes one think of comfortable things like sweet-scented clover and hay-fields and honey-comb and shining golden honey trickling out of a silver spoon.

But there is an old story about bees that is

7

told in Japan, which has nothing to do with such things as these. It tells of a very great Swarm of Bees that was so powerful that it put to flight an army. It is the story of Yogodagu and the Bees of Yamato.

Long ago, almost a thousand years ago, lived Yogodagu, a prince and a warrior of Japan. He built a strong castle in a wild and lonely part of the province of Yamato, and there he lived and ruled the country-side.

But a powerful enemy came against him with an army, and in a battle Yogodagu and his followers were defeated. Yogodagu and twenty of his men escaped, and they fled away and came by night to a little valley deep among the mountains of Kasagi. There they hid themselves in a cave among the rocks and trees, and rested, and bound up their wounds.

They were afraid that their enemies had followed them even there ; but a whole day passed and there was no sign or sound of armed men. Another day came and went safely, and at sunrise on the third day Yogodagu came boldly out of his hiding-place and stood looking up and down the valley.

He was wounded. He was hungry and weary. He had no home. His friends and followers were scattered far and wide, and his enemy was hunting him like a wild beast. Yet, as Yogodagu stood there on that morning of early summer, he was not thinking of his sorrows and troubles and fears. He smiled to himself for joy.

" Yamato is a very fair land," he said.

The valley was indeed most beautiful. It lay in shadow, for the sun had not yet climbed above the mountain-tops ; but overhead the sky was blue, and behind the eastern hills was golden light. The south wind rustled softly among the young green leaves and set the flowers nodding in the grass. It was a lovely, peaceful place.

As Yogodagu watched, the sun climbed higher in the sky and looked down into the valley. It touched the tree tops and lit the mountain-side. The leaves of the oaks were golden in the morning light. The young shoots of the maples were tipped with crimson. The wild wistaria hung in long trails of misty blue among the branches. The bamboos shone like emeralds, and the azaleas were like clouds at sunset, pink and amber and orange and rose.

Presently, as he stood there, Yogodagu noticed that a cluster of flowers on a bush near-by was nodding and shaking as if it were being tossed by a little wind. He moved closer and stooped to look. Then he saw that a great spider had spun its web from flower to flower, and into the web had blundered a little brown bee. It was struggling to escape, and in its struggles it shook the web and the rosy azalea flowers, while the spider sat watching and waiting to seize it when it should be too tired to sting.

" My honourable little friend," said Yogodagu to the bee, " I too have an enemy who watches and waits to kill me, and it seems that

I may not be able to escape. But I can set you free to fly."

As he said this he bent down and broke the web and carefully lifted the bee with a twig and set it in the cup of a flower. Then he

stood watching while it cleaned itself from the sticky clinging strands of web, till it spread its wings and darted away like a little shining spark in the sunlight.

Yogodagu sighed, and wished that he could come and go as freely and happily as the little brown bee. All that day he thought and planned, but there seemed no way of escape for him and his faithful men.

Chapter Two : Yogodagu's Dream

Now that night, as Yogodagu slept, he dreamed a dream. He thought that as he stood in the valley a man came to him, a little man in brown and gold with a sharp and shining dagger at his side.

" Honourable Sir," said the man, " I am the bee whom you helped. Now in my turn I will help you. There are millions of bees in

Yamato, and all will come at my call. This you must do. Build in this valley a house to shelter you and your men, and round it build a wall that will shelter the bees. Have no fear. My people will fight for you in time of need, and you shall escape your enemy."

Yogodagu awoke. The sun was climbing above the mountain tops. The wind was rustling among the trees. He remembered how he had walked among the flowers, and how he had let the little bee go free. He thought of the dream that had come to him in the night, and he resolved to follow the bee-man's advice.

So, at the end of the valley, he and his men built a little house to shelter them. Round it they made a wall of hollow logs and stones and stumps of trees, all loosely piled together to make a dwelling for the bees. When all was ready, the bees came. From hollow rocks and trees, from caves and crevices in the mountain sides, from far and near they came in buzzing swarms, and settled in the place that Yogodagu had made for them. More and more came, till all day long the air was filled with the sound of their humming wings. Even by night their soft and sleepy murmur could be heard—thousands and thousands of bees, all guarding the house of Yogodagu.

One day a messenger came running from a friendly village with news for Yogodagu. His enemy had heard of the house in the valley, and he was on his way with a band of men to drive Yogodagu from that shelter, as he had driven him from his castle and his lands.

The messenger begged Yogodagu to fly farther into the mountains, but Yogodagu refused. He remembered the bee-man's promise and he did not try to escape.

When his enemy with his army came to the valley they saw Yogodagu and his men standing before their house. They looked ready to fight. Their spears shone in the sunlight and their bows were drawn.

But as the enemy drew near, it seemed that Yogodagu's men were only cowards after all. They shot a few arrows and then turned and ran into the house. The enemy's men shouted. Their leader laughed.

" Charge ! " he shouted. " Break down their miserable wall. Kill Yogodagu, and scatter his men like dead leaves in autumn."

His men rushed forward. Up to the clumsy wall they came. They crashed into it. Down went the wall, and up from its ruins, with a roar of wings, rose a great dark cloud of bees. Thousands and thousands there were. The air was black with them.

In one moment the enemy's army turned and fled, and behind them came the angry Bees of Yamato.

What happened to the leader the story does not say, but his army was scattered far and wide, and never again did he trouble Yogodagu. Yogodagu with his men went back to the castle from which they had been driven, and lived there happily for many years to come.

He did not forget his faithful friends, the bees. When the battle was over he and his men gathered up the little brown bodies.

Thousands of them had fallen in the fight, for bees nearly always die after they sting. They hurt themselves more than they hurt their enemy.

These they buried in one grave, and over it they built a temple. Year by year, when the month of May came round, Yogodagu journeyed to the little valley among the mountains. There he prayed and made offerings, and gave thanks in the temple that he had built in remembrance of that brave army, the little brown Bees of Yamato.

THE BAD LITTLE JACKAL

Chapter One : Dry Days

A JACKAL is rather like a fox. He has a sharp nose, pricked-up ears, a bushy tail, and a coat which is sometimes yellowish-grey and sometimes rather brown. He is clever and cunning and mean and greedy, and is fond of picking up scraps and stealing other people's food instead of hunting for himself. He is always up to tricks, and so was the jackal in our story. He lived in South Africa, and the tale has been told there for many a day.

One year it was terribly hot in Africa. No rain fell. The grass and trees died, and nearly all the rivers and pools dried up. The animals were terribly thirsty, and went about with their tongues hanging out.

But at last rain came. The pools and rivers filled. The grass and trees were green, and the animals grew fat and strong.

Then they said to one another, " Now, if we are wise, we shall make a plan to store up water before the next dry time comes. Then we may have plenty to drink."

So they all met together. Lion was there, and Ostrich, Ant-eater, Baboon, Rabbit, Deer, little Tortoise, and many others.

Jackal came too.

After talking for a long while they made up their minds to find a place where there was a spring. There they were going to dig a large deep hole for the water to trickle into. Then there would be a great pool to drink from, no matter how long it was before the rain fell again.

" Will you all agree to dig ? " said Lion in his deep voice.

" Oh yes, Uncle," they all said. (They

18

called him " Uncle " because he was such a great lion.)

" Oh yes, Uncle," they all said again, and Jackal joined in too.

" Oh yes, *indeed*, Uncle," said Jackal.

Chapter Two : How the Well was Made

So they all began to dig.

Lion scratched with his forepaws and kicked with his hind legs, and made the sand fly.

Ostrich scratched.

Ant-eater dug busily with his paws and claws.

Even little Sister Tortoise dug with her little feet.

Everybody did their best, except Jackal. What do you suppose he did ? He sat and laughed.

" Work ? " said Jackal. " Not I. You work and I will drink when you have finished."

This made the animals cross, because they knew he would do as he said. He was always stealing their food, and now he meant to steal their water.

They were very angry, but no one wasted time trying to answer him. They went on digging, while Jackal laughed and said rude things.

By and by the deep pool was finished, and the clear cool water flowed into it and filled it to the brim.

" Now," said Lion, " we will build a high wall round it and leave a narrow gate. Then we will set a guard to watch. Jackal would not help to dig the pool, and he shall not drink the water. That is quite fair, I am sure you will all agree."

Soon the wall was built.

" Now," said Lion, " who will guard the gate ? "

" I will, Uncle ! I will ! " said Hare.

" Very well," said Lion. " Hare is small and quick. He has big eyes that see well in the dark."

All the animals thought it would be a good plan, so they said Good night and went away to their homes.

Chapter Three : Poor Mr. Hare !

HARE sat by the opening and watched with his big eyes. He was thinking what a fine fellow he was and how he would chase Jackal with his long legs if he even came near the well.

Presently he saw Jackal strolling quietly past, nibbling something. As Jackal came near, Hare saw it was a piece of honeycomb.

Jackal did not seem to see Hare at all. He strolled along, nibbling and singing a little song. Presently he stopped and leaned against the wall, quite close to Hare. " How  *nice* it is ! " he said to himself. " How *sweet* it is ! I am not thirsty. How could I be, with this sweet clear honey to drink ? "

Hare watched him nibble, and wondered if it really was so very good.

At last he said, " Is it so very good, Jackal ? "

" Oh, are you there ? " said Jackal. " I did not see you. Yes, it is very good. As for water, who cares about that, if they can get honey ? "

" Could I taste it ? " said Hare.

" Well," said Jackal, " I would let you taste it, but you have been put there by those angry animals to guard the water. How am I to know that you won't hurt me if I come near you ? "

" I won't hurt you," said Hare.

" Well," said Jackal, " let me tie your paws, and then I will put the honey into your mouth."

" Oh yes, indeed," said silly Hare. He thought to himself, " Jackal does not really want any water at all."

Jackal tied Hare's paws so that he could not move. Then he just jumped over him and splashed into the cool clear pool.

He swam round and round. He drank all he could. Then he stirred up the mud and ran away laughing, leaving a dirty pool behind him. He did not even give Hare one taste of honey.

When the animals came to drink that evening their beautiful water was all muddy, and Hare was tied up like a bundle. They were so cross that they quarrelled about who should guard the pool next. They were very rude to each other.

When everyone had finished making a noise, little Sister Tortoise said in her quiet voice, " I can guard the water."

As they were all rather ashamed of having been angry and foolish, they agreed to let her do it.

So little Sister Tortoise sat herself in the opening. She tucked her head into her shell and drew in her feet and her tail till no one could tell which end of her was which. Then she waited.

Chapter Four : Sister Tortoise Keeps Guard

PRESENTLY Sister Tortoise heard Jackal coming, singing his little song and nibbling his sweet honeycomb. He looked all round with his sharp eyes. There was only quiet little

Sister Tortoise to be seen, and she neither moved nor spoke.

" Will you have some sweet honey, Sister Tortoise ? " said Jackal.

But Sister Tortoise stayed inside her shell and never spoke.

" Do have some sweet honey," said Jackal ; but Sister Tortoise was quite quiet. Jackal really could not tell if he was talking to her head or tail.

" Silly thing ! " said Jackal. " She is asleep. I need not trouble about her. I will go and enjoy the water again."

He was just stepping over Sister Tortoise, when out came her little head and she caught Jackal by the hind leg. How Jackal squealed !

How he kicked ! He begged Sister Tortoise to let go. He offered her all his honey. He promised her juicy green grass and leaves to eat. He cried and he sobbed, but still she held on.

Hour after hour went by. Jackal had time to think how angry the animals would be, and what dreadful things they would do to him when they came in the evening to drink and found him there.

" I thought I was too clever for any of them," he moaned, " and I have been caught by quiet little Sister Tortoise."

Then he stopped thinking. They were coming.

Chapter Five : Good-bye, Mr. Jackal

BUT when they saw Jackal looking so funny, all they could do was to sit and laugh.

Lion roared, so did Ostrich. The others chuckled and squealed and shrieked. Jackal hated it. He could not bear being laughed at. At last he could stand it no longer, and he gave one last kick.

Perhaps Sister Tortoise was sorry for him, for she let go and laughed too. As for Jackal, he ran and ran and ran and ran. Far away he went, and never came back to spoil that nice

pool any more. After that all the animals used to come every evening to bathe and drink at their beautiful pool. They were all very grateful to little Sister Tortoise.

Chapter One : The Drowsy Fairy

THERE was once a man who caught a fairy.

His name was Master Jacob Pigginpound, and he had a little farm and a little house where he lived with his wife, Mistress Martha Pigginpound.

Early in the morning, one day in June, Master Jacob went out to the pasture to drive the cows in for milking, and there, right in the middle of an ox-eye daisy and fast asleep, lay the fairy. He had been dancing all night on a fairy ring, and he was so tired that he had climbed up the stalk of the daisy and had laid himself down to rest a little, and had fallen fast asleep on its yellow middle.

Some people would have thought it was a lovely thing to find a fairy. But Master Jacob only thought of what he could get. And he picked up the poor fairy between his big finger and thumb and carried him into the house, still half asleep.

" Wife," he said, " I have caught a fairy."

Mistress Martha begged him to let the fairy go among the flowers in the garden.

" Put the poor little dear in the red rose bush, or among the pinks, or into a Canterbury bell, Jacob, do," she said.

But Master Jacob shook his head and fetched a big blue-and-white mug and popped the fairy in. " There you shall stay," he said, " till I hear what you will give me to let you go."

Then he put a saucer on the top and stood the mug on the kitchen dresser. Mistress Martha did not dare to touch it. She knew Master Jacob would be angry if she meddled. So there the poor Fairy had to stay all that day, while out of doors the sun shone, the birds sang, and the tall white daisies and the buttercups and the grass and the red sorrel nodded and danced as the wind blew over the hayfields.

"WIFE, " HE SAID, " I HAVE CAUGHT A FAIRY."

In the evening, when Master Jacob had finished his day's work and had come home to get his tea, he lifted the saucer off the mug and said, " Well, Master Fairy, what is it to be ? "

The Fairy said in a small, clear voice, " You shall find a piece of gold at the end of every furrow that you plough."

Then he jumped, just like a grasshopper, very quick and sudden, straight out of the mug, right over Master Jacob's head, on to the window-ledge, and out of the kitchen window into Mistress Martha's bed of pinks that grew just outside the house.

" And a good thing too, poor little creature," said Mistress Martha.

Chapter Two : The Promise Comes True

JACOB said nothing at all. He forgot all about his tea. He was out of the house in a minute, and he harnessed a horse to the plough and drove a furrow right down the middle of the pasture field where the cows were feeding.

Sure enough, at the end of the furrow there lay a shining gold piece. He went on ploughing till the moon was high in the sky. By that time half the green pasture field was turned to brown furrows, and Master Jacob had a pocket full of gold pieces.

After that Jacob did nothing but plough. As soon as his fields were ploughed, he ploughed them again. Nothing grew on his farm, for he neither planted nor sowed ; he only picked up gold pieces and stored them away. He sold his cows. He ploughed up his garden, his pastures and his cornfields. He grew thin and bent and weary with ploughing. He was afraid his gold would be stolen, so he never spoke to his neighbours, and he let no one come near the house. He could never bear to spend his precious gold, and he and poor Mistress Martha had scarcely enough to eat.

So the time passed, and June came round again. One day Mistress Martha stood at the door of the house looking out at the little farm. She shook her head and almost cried as she looked. The garden was gone. There were no more pinks or roses or Canterbury bells. There were no lavender bushes, no vegetable garden with tidy green rows of carrots and potatoes and peas. The green grass was gone too; so were the hayfields and the fields of clover and young green corn. There was nothing but bare brown earth; and in the distance she could see Master Jacob toiling after a plough and stooping at the end of each furrow to pick up his piece of gold.

" Bless the man ! " said Mistress Martha.

" There he goes, working all day and half the night. The house is full of bags of gold, and both of us are just as miserable as can be. I wish we could go back to last June, I do, so happy and comfortable as we were ! "

Just at that moment Mistress Martha heard a loud cackling behind the house. Then another hen joined in with more loud cackling.

" I do believe those hens have been laying," she said. " I don't know what's been wrong with them lately. I have had no eggs at all. I will go and see."

She bustled round to the hen-house and came back again with two beautiful big brown eggs.

" I do declare," she said, " I will boil these eggs for tea. A new-laid egg will be a treat and do us good. So it will."

She stood by the door, watching for a moment, with the two brown eggs in her hand. Just as she turned to go into the house the garden gate clicked. A little lame old man with a pedlar's pack upon his back came hobbling up the path.

Chapter Three : The Lame Pedlar Man

" WHERE ever did he come from ? " Mistress Martha said to herself. " I never saw him coming up the road. I suppose the sun was in my eyes."

" It is no use your coming here," she said to the Pedlar. " I have no money to spend on ribbons or laces nowadays, or needles and pins and tapes either, for that matter.

" Let me rest a minute, mistress," said the little old man. " I am old, and the pack is heavy. Could you spare me a drink of water ? It is a hot day, and the road is dusty."

" Sit down on the step," said Mistress Martha, " and let your pack down to rest your back. You shall have the water and welcome."

33

She fetched the water, all cool and fresh from the well, in the same blue-and-white mug that Master Jacob had put the fairy in. Then, because the Pedlar looked so old and tired, she stepped back into the kitchen and took the brown egg that she was going to have for her own tea, and laid it carefully in the pack, all among the pink and blue ribbons and the handkerchiefs and laces.

" There you are," she said. " I wish I had more to give."

" Thank you, mistress," said the old man, " with all my heart. One good turn, they say, deserves another. So take a dip from my lucky bag before I go."

He held out a little bag that looked as if all the colours of the rainbow had been woven into it. It was as green as grass, as red as poppies in the corn, as yellow as buttercups, and as blue as the summer sky, with every colour you can think of in between. Mistress Martha put her fingers in, but all she could feel was a soft powdery stuff.

34

"Take a pinch and smell it," said the little old man.

Mistress Martha sniffed. It was so sweet that she shut her eyes to smell it better. "It is like the pinks that used to grow under the kitchen window," she said.

She sniffed again.

"No, it is like the lavender bushes that grew by the garden path."

She sniffed again.

"It is like the big red rose bush that grew by the gate," she said, and sniffed again, a very big sniff.

She was going to say, "It's like mint and thyme and sage and southernwood," but she never said any of it. She only sneezed.

"At-choo," said Mistress Martha, "at-choo—a-*tish*-oo!"

She shut her eyes tighter than ever when she sneezed. Most people do. When she opened them, the Pedlar was gone. But Mistress Martha had no time to be surprised at that: she was so busy looking with all her eyes.

35

Chapter Four : Master Jacob Wakes Up

FOR what do you think ? It really was the pinks under the kitchen window that were smelling so sweet ; and the lavender bushes with their grey-green leaves and blue-grey flowers ; and the big red rose bush that grew by the gate. There they all were, and all the other flowers too. There were the mint and thyme and southernwood, the carrots and turnips and potatoes and peas.

Mistress Martha rubbed her eyes and looked, and then she looked again. The pasture was there, and so were the cows. In the field beyond, the young green wheat was growing, and she could see the hayfield rippling in the wind. And there was Master Jacob coming whistling up the road, just as he used to come before he found the fairy and shut it up in the blue-and-white mug.

" Bless me ! " said Mistress Martha, and she turned round and looked in at the kitchen window. There was a beautiful tea on the table : a currant loaf, white bread and brown bread, yellow butter and creamy cheese, and streaky pink-and-white bacon. The kettle was boiling on the fire, and the big brown teapot was standing on the hob.

" Bless me ! " said Mistress Martha, and she ran upstairs and looked in the box under the bed.

The bags of gold were gone. There was only Master Jacob's big leather purse with the money for market day.

The queerest thing of all was that when

Master Jacob came in, and washed himself, and sat down to his tea, he seemed to have forgotten all about the fairy and the fairy gold. He ate his tea and enjoyed it. Then he said :

" Wife, we will go to market to-morrow and buy you a new dress. You look a bit tired, and a change will do you good."

When they got to market everybody else

37

had forgotten about Master Jacob's ploughing and his sour ways too. Mistress Martha had a new dress of a beautiful blue, just like periwinkle flowers, and she felt so happy and excited about it that she began to forget as well. Quite soon the only person who remembered was the fairy. He was very careful never to go to sleep in the middle of an ox-eye daisy again.

And who do *you* think the Pedlar was?

The TALE of KING SOLOMON and the HOOPOE

Chapter One :
Shade in the Desert

HERE is an old tale that the Arabs tell of Solomon, the great King of the Jews. Besides being a great ruler, King Solomon made books of wise sayings, and sweet songs to sing, and wrote down all that he could learn of trees and plants, from the great cedar of Lebanon to the little green plants that grew between the stones of his palace walls. He gathered all he could hear of beasts and birds too, and of creeping things and fishes. He loved to know all that could be known of everything that lived.

In the days of King Solomon very few people troubled themselves about such things, and it seemed very strange to them that he should trouble his head about them. In the end they came to believe that Solomon by his magic could talk to all creatures and make them do his will. That was how the tale of the Hoopoe began.

First of all, do you know what a Hoopoe is ? He is a bird—a small bird with a long sharp beak. He is rather bigger than a thrush, but he has longer and stronger legs than a thrush because he likes running better than flying. His wings and his tail are striped across with black and white. His head and his neck are a beautiful colour, almost golden ; I think they would look like old gold in the sunlight. And on his head—but you must wait till the end of the story to know about that.

This is the story :

One day King Solomon was riding in a wild and lonely place on the edge of the desert. He was on his way home, and he was very hot and tired. It was summer-time, and as the sun climbed higher and higher in the blue sky, its rays beat down upon the King till he longed to be in his palace in Jerusalem, with its cool dark rooms and its splashing fountains. But Jerusalem was far away, and Solomon was almost fainting with the heat. He looked round for shelter ; but there was no shade to be seen, not a tree, not even a great rock. There were only low prickly bushes, hot sand and pebbles, and patches of dusty ground covered with burnt-up grass.

Presently a great flock of birds came flying like a cloud across the desert. Just for a moment, as the flock passed overhead, its shadow fell upon King Solomon and gave a cool and pleasant shade. As the birds flew on, and their shadow skimmed over the ground beneath, Solomon said to himself :

" I will call my friends, the birds of the desert, to help me."

He looked round to see which of them was near ; and there, quite close to him, was the Hoopoe, pecking and scratching happily on a pebbly sandy bit of ground. He was rather bigger than a thrush, but with longer and stronger legs, so that he liked running better than flying.

His golden head and neck were very much the colour of golden sand in the hot bright sunshine, and his black-and-white wings and tail looked wonderfully like a heap of stones and pebbles, so that he was not easy to see.

But Solomon saw him in a moment. " Oh, little friend Hoopoe," he said, " call your brothers and bid them fly like a thick cloud between me and the sun, so that I may have shelter from the heat."

" O Lord King," said the Hoopoe, " most certainly I will."

Then he gave his queer little cry, that sounds like " Ooop-ooo, ooop-ooo," and called his friends. They all came, and, spreading their wings, they flew between King Solomon and the sun, and sheltered him from the heat.

So the King rode on in comfort, all through the weary hot hours of the day, till the shadows began to stretch out longer and longer, and he knew that the cool of the evening was near.

Presently a little breeze began to blow, and he stopped his horse and called to the Hoopoes.

" Come now, my friends," he cried. " Tell me, what shall I give to you as thanks and a

blessing for your great kindness to me this day ?"

As they heard his call, the Hoopoes wheeled in the air and came sweeping to the ground.

Folding their wings, they sat round King Solomon. Then they all looked at the Hoopoe who had called them.

" You speak for us," they seemed to be saying, because they were rather shy.

The Hoopoe looked down at the ground and scratched bashfully with his little claws. He was feeling shy, too, about what he was going

to say. But at last he looked up at King Solomon and said :

" O Lord King, all the time that we have been flying above you, we have admired the beautiful shining golden crown that you wear upon your head. Grant, if you will, that all

Hoopoes may wear shining golden crowns like yours, O King!"

No wonder he was bashful about asking!

King Solomon looked rather sadly at the Hoopoe.

"Little brother," he said, "is there nothing else that will please you as well as a crown of gold?"

"Nothing, my Lord King," the Hoopoe said very firmly, to show that he had quite made up his mind, and it was no use arguing with him.

"Then you and all Hoopoes shall have golden crowns," said the King. As he spoke he raised his hand. At once on the head of every Hoopoe there was a little shining crown of gold, most beautiful to see.

"But remember," said Solomon, "remember, O little friends of mine, that your crowns may bring you sorrow instead of joy. In seven days from now I will come again to this place, and you shall tell me if your wish is still the same."

But the Hoopoes scarcely listened to him:

they were admiring each other so much. They could hardly wait to thank the King properly, before flying away helter-skelter to show all the other birds and beasts and insects how grand they were. King Solomon watched them go, and sighed a little, and rode back to his palace in Jerusalem.

Chapter Two : All is not gold——

THE Hoopoe who had asked for the crowns flew home as fast as he could go. He wanted to get back to his wife, who was tucked away in a hollow tree, sitting on a nest full of eggs. She was hungry and rather cross, because she had been waiting all the afternoon to be fed. She poked her head out of a little hole in the tree trunk when she heard him coming. But just as she was beginning to scold him she caught sight of his golden crown.

" Why, Father Hoopoe," she said, " what is that curious thing upon your head ? "

" Don't you admire it, my dear ? " said Father Hoopoe ; and he told her all about his afternoon's work, and how all Hoopoes had been given shining golden crowns by the great King.

" Have I got one on my head ? " asked Mother Hoopoe.

" Yes, my love," said Father Hoopoe. " All our folk are wearing them now."

" Then I don't like it at all," said Mother Hoopoe. " It is not as comfortable as feathers. I wondered why my head felt so heavy. Besides, Father Hoopoe, do you think it is wise to wear anything so bright ? "

" I don't know what you mean, my dear," said Father Hoopoe crossly. " It is most beautiful and becoming. Now let me get a wink of sleep. I am too tired to talk any more after all that flying."

But at the bottom of his heart he was not quite so sure as he had been that a golden crown was really the best thing for a little bird to wear. And when morning came, and he went out to peck and scratch for food, he soon found that Mother Hoopoe was right. His feathers had been exactly the thing to hide him, for they were so much the colour of the sand and stones that he could hardly be seen. But a shining golden crown is very easy to see in the sunlight, and poor Father Hoopoe had never had so many narrow escapes as on that day.

Hawks swooped down at him, and he had to hide among thorn bushes. A jackal pounced at him, and he only just fluttered away in time. Worst of all, a shepherd boy with a sling chased him with stones wherever he went. He had very hard work to find enough food for Mother Hoopoe and himself, and by evening he was very tired and miserable. All his friends were unhappy, too, and the next day it was worse. Folk with slings and sticks and stones seemed to be everywhere. The shepherd boy had spread the news of the birds with the golden crowns, and from far and near men came to hunt them down.

Luckily Mother Hoopoe and her nest were well hidden away in the hollow tree, so she was safe. But she was nearly starved, poor thing. Father Hoopoe scarcely dared show the tip of his long beak to look for food.

A SHEPHERD BOY WITH A SLING CHASED HIM WITH STONES.

At last the evening of the seventh day came.

" Now, my dear," said Mother Hoopoe, " do go and ask the King to take the nasty things off our heads and let us have a little peace. I have hardly had a wink of sleep for worrying about you, and it is time we both had a little more food."

" Yes, my love," said poor tired Father Hoopoe in a weak voice. " I certainly will."

He flew away to the place where he had last seen King Solomon. There sat the great King on his horse, waiting, and from far and near Hoopoes came flying to meet him. Their golden crowns shone in the sunlight, but their feathers were draggled and ruffled ; and there were not nearly so many Hoopoes as before.

King Solomon looked at them sadly.

" O little friends," he said, " are you happy with your crowns ? "

All the Hoopoes answered together :

" Take away our golden crowns, O King ! Take away our golden crowns ! "

" I will," Solomon said. " Crowns of gold are not for birds to wear. But because you are the friends of a King, and gave him help in time of need, every one of you shall wear the crown of a king ; but it shall be of feathers, not of gold."

As he spoke he raised his hand. The

Hoopoes looked at each other, and on every Hoopoe's head was a little crown of feathers, gold-coloured and tipped with black.

This time they really thanked King Solomon properly. They pattered round him on the sand. They bowed and scraped and piped their little call of " Ooop-ooo, ooop-ooo " again and again. They thanked him in every way they knew. At last the wise King smiled, and blessed them, and sent them away to their homes.

Father Hoopoe flew straight back to Mother Hoopoe.

She popped her head, with a little feather crown on it, out of the hollow tree when she heard him coming. When she saw him she was perfectly delighted.

" My dear love," she said, " how charmingly distinguished! And what very good taste! "

" Yes, my dear," said Father Hoopoe, " and so safe! "

Then he flew happily away to find some food for himself and Mother Hoopoe before the sun went down.

To this day the Hoopoe wears upon his head a tiny crown in memory of the kindness of King Solomon the Wise.

THE DOG-BROTHER

HERE is an old story and a true one. It happened in the year 1426 in the part of the world which is now called Asia Minor.

It is the story of a dog.

His name has been forgotten, but he was a real dog—a great hound with a smooth dark coat and long drooping ears. His home was in a great castle that stood high on a rocky cliff above the blue Mediterranean, a stronghold of the Knights of St. John. There had been war for more than three hundred years between the Christians and the Turks, and none had fought more bravely in that war than these Knights.

Year after year men came from all the noble families of Europe and joined them, and promised to give their lives to fight against the Turks. Many were killed, but there were always more ready to guard Europe and to hold back the Tartars from the east and the Turks from the south, who would have liked to take the rich lands round the Mediterranean for their own.

The castle stood not far from the country of the Turks. It had been built as a place of refuge for the Christian prisoners whom the Turks sometimes took in battle and kept as slaves and treated very cruelly. So it was made very strong, with seven walls on the landward side and seven ramparts on the seaward side. Over the gateway of the castle these words were carved: "Except the Lord keep the House, his labour is but lost that buildeth," and it was called St. Peter of the Freed, because it was for men to come to and be free.

Many slaves did escape to the castle, and were cared for and sent safely back to their homes. But some who tried to reach it lost their way among the hills and mountains, and died of hunger and cold and weariness. So the good Brothers of St. John, as they were sometimes called, trained hounds to go out into the mountains to search for lost travellers and to guide them safely to the castle. Our dog was one of these.

One day a man named Francisco escaped from his Turkish master and started on his journey through the mountain-country to reach St. Peter of the Freed. He hurried as fast as he was able, because he was terribly afraid of being caught. He knew his master would come after him with men on horseback, who could go faster than he could ; and if he were taken he would be beaten and cruelly punished, perhaps even killed.

So, as he ran, he looked for a place where he could hide safely until they were tired of searching for him—a cave in the rocks, a tree to climb, or a village where people would be kind and help him. But there seemed no caves or trees, and there were no villages, for all the people had been driven away by the Turks.

Francisco was beginning to feel very tired and frightened, when, as he hurried along, he came to a place among the mountains where once there had been a village, but now there were only **brok**en-down walls and ruined

houses. He ran in and out among them, looking for a hiding-place ; but nowhere seemed safe till he came to a hole in the ground which looked deep and dark.

By this time he was terribly frightened, for he was sure he could hear men coming. So he did not wait to see how deep it was, but caught hold of the edge and dropped. The hole was much deeper than he thought, for it had been a well, though fortunately there was no longer any water in it. But he was not hurt, and he felt very glad to be so safely hidden ; for as he crouched there at the bottom of the well he could hear the sound of horses' hoofs, and men talking and shouting. He knew that it was his master's servants. He had been only just in time.

They went all through the ruined village, calling to each other as they searched, but no one thought of looking in the well ; and at last they went away to follow the path still farther into the mountains.

Francisco stayed where he was, for he knew they would return that way. Presently he heard them coming back, very angry because they had not found him. But this time they went straight through the village, and he heard the sound of their horses' hoofs die away in the distance.

" Now I will climb out," he said to himself, " and make my way to the castle of St. Peter of the Freed. The good Brothers of St. John will keep me safe and send me back to my home."

He began to try to climb the side of the well. But it was much harder than he expected : it

THEY WERE SURE HE DID NOT EAT IT, FOR HE WAS GROWING
THIN.

was steep and slippery; there seemed no place to put his foot and nothing for his hands to hold to. He tried again and again, all round the walls of the well. Sometimes he climbed a little way, but each time he slipped and fell, till at last he was so tired that he fell asleep.

When he woke it was night, and the great bright stars were shining. He was stiff and sore and aching, but he tried again and again, till at last he was quite sure. The well was so steep that unless someone let down a rope to him he could never get out; and who could come to help him in that lonely place? After all, he thought, he would never go home as he had hoped. He was very frightened and very miserable.

The night went by and day came, and presently Francisco heard a pattering. Then there was a sound of scratching and snuffling at the mouth of the well. He saw the head of some animal looking down into the well. It was a great dog.

Francisco thought some hunter or shepherd must be near, and he called and shouted. But

57

no one came, and presently the big dog trotted away. Francisco felt even more frightened and lonely than before, because he really had begun to hope a little. So the day passed and night came, and by now he was terribly hungry. He knew that if no help came he must soon die. But help did come.

For when morning broke, Francisco heard the quick-pattering feet again, and saw the great dog looking down into the well. But this time it carried something in its mouth, and it dropped what it carried into the well. It was a piece of meat. It was raw meat, the dog's own breakfast. But Francisco was so hungry that he ate it and was glad. He felt his strength coming back and he knew he would not die of hunger that day.

After that, day by day, the great dog came to the well bringing a piece of meat, and it kept Francisco alive.

But in the castle of St. Peter of the Freed the good Brothers of St. John were troubled about one of their dogs. Instead of eating his food he always picked it up and trotted away with it. No one knew where he went, but they were sure he did not eat it, for he was growing thin and his coat was rough. They were afraid he was ill, and it troubled them, because they loved their dogs.

So one day some of the Brothers followed to see where he went. He went a long long way,

up rocky hillsides, down mountain valleys, and along steep narrow paths, till he came to a place where once there had been a village but now there were only broken-down walls and ruined houses.

They saw the dog go trotting in and out among the ruins, till he stopped at what looked like a deep hole and dropped the meat he was carrying down into it. Then they ran to the hole and leaned over to look what was there. A faint voice was calling. They knew there was a man in the hole. They called to him that help was coming ; and while one stayed by the well, so that Francisco might not feel he was left all alone, the others hurried back across the mountains and brought a strong rope.

They lowered a man down into the well, and he put his arms round Francisco and held him safe, because he was very weak and could not hold the rope for himself, and they were pulled out of the well together. Then they carried Francisco back to the castle of St. Peter of the Freed, and nursed and cared for him till he was able to go safely home.

But when the Chronicler of the Order of the Knights of St. John of Jerusalem heard what the dog had done, he took the great book in which the history of the Order was written. It was a great book bound in leather, with clasps of brass and crackling pages of parchment, and on those pages in thick black writing were all the stories of the noble doings of the Knights of St. John of Jerusalem.

The Chronicler took his pen, and dipped it in the ink and wrote the story of the dog. If anyone had said to him, " Why do you write the story of a dog among the deeds of the Knights of the great Order of St. John of Jerusalem ? " he would have said, " Surely he too is worthy to be called a Brother of our Order, for he too went out into the wilderness and gave all that he had, that he might seek and save that which was lost."

That is why this story is called " The Story of the Dog-Brother of the Order of St. John of Jerusalem."

QUESTIONS

YOGODAGU AND THE BEES OF YAMATO (page 7)

1. What was Yamato, and what do you know about it ?
2. In what country did the bees live ? Name some of the trees and flowers.
3. Why did the bees like Yogodagu ?
4. What sort of a house was it that his men built ?
5. Tell his dream and how it came true.
6. Look at the picture on page 11 and talk about Yogodagu's dress and moustache. Next tell how a Japanese general dressed in those days.

THE BAD LITTLE JACKAL (page 17)

1. What is a jackal like to look at ?
2. What is he like in his ways ?
3. What do you know about hare's eyes ?
4. What are the animals doing in the picture on page 17 ? What is that one with the bushiest tail ?
5. What animals can you see on page 26 ?

THE TALE OF THE FARMER AND THE FAIRY (page 27)

1. Look at the left half of the picture on page 27. What is there in it that you might overlook if you had not read the story ?
2. Draw the ox-eye daisy as it was when Master Jacob saw it first.
3. About how long did the fairy stay in the mug ? How do you know ?
4. Why did Master Jacob give up growing things ?
5. Suppose that you are Mistress Martha, sitting looking out over the bare garden and writing a letter to your sister. Write it.

6. How do you know that Jacob had forgotten the fairy ?

7. Draw the answer to the question on page 38.

8. Tell what sort of clothes Master Jacob and his wife wore.

THE TALE OF KING SOLOMON AND THE HOOPOE (page 39)

1. What was King Solomon's hobby ?　What is yours ?

2. Paint a picture of a hoopoe.

3. Why are hoopoe's called by that name ?

4. Why is a hoopoe not easy to see in the desert ?　Say anything you know about other creatures which are protected in that way.

5. Why were crowns bad for the hoopoes ?

6. Tell how the King was dressed indoors, and when he went riding.

7. Finish the saying that makes the title of Chapter Two. What does it mean ?　Would Father Hoopoe have thought it true ?　Perhaps you can tell another tale with that saying for a title.

THE DOG-BROTHER (page 52)

1. Why did the Knights build the castle, and why did they fight ?

2. What was the castle called, and why ?

3. Why did they keep hounds ?

4. How did the Knights know that the dog was not eating his food ?

5. How did they have to get the slave up, and why ?

6. Out of what book did the story first come ?

7. What was the motto over the castle gate ?　What does it mean ?